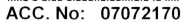

For Milly and Sophie x

First published in 2020 by Child's Play (International) Ltd
Ashworth Road, Bridgemead, Swindon SN5 7YD, UK

First published in USA in 2020 by Child's Play Inc
250 Minot Avenue, Auburn, Maine 04210

Distributed in Australia by Child's Play Australia Pty Ltd
Unit 10/20 Narabang Way, Belrose, Sydney, NSW 2085

Text copyright © 2020 Susan Rollings
Illustrations copyright © 2020 Child's Play (International) Ltd
The moral rights of the author and illustrator have been asserted

ISBN 978-1-78628-467-9
SJ200320CPL04204679

Printed in Shenzhen, China

1 3 5 7 9 10 8 6 4 2

A catalogue record of this book
is available from the British Library

www.childs-play.com

New Shoes, Red Shoes

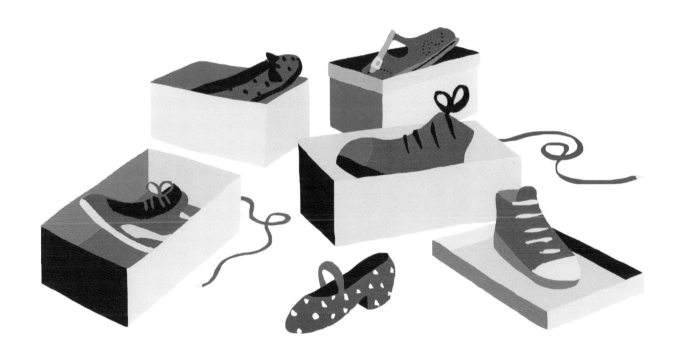

Susan Rollings   illustrated by Becky Baur

Two shoes, small shoes,
off to get some new shoes.

Skipping shoes, hopping shoes,

waiting for the bus shoes.

High shoes, low shoes,

riding on the bus shoes.

Summer shoes, strappy shoes,

playing in the park shoes.

Friends' shoes, comfy shoes,

tiny little baby shoes.

Strong shoes, tough shoes,

working hard to build shoes.

Busy shoes, shopping shoes,

are we nearly there shoes?

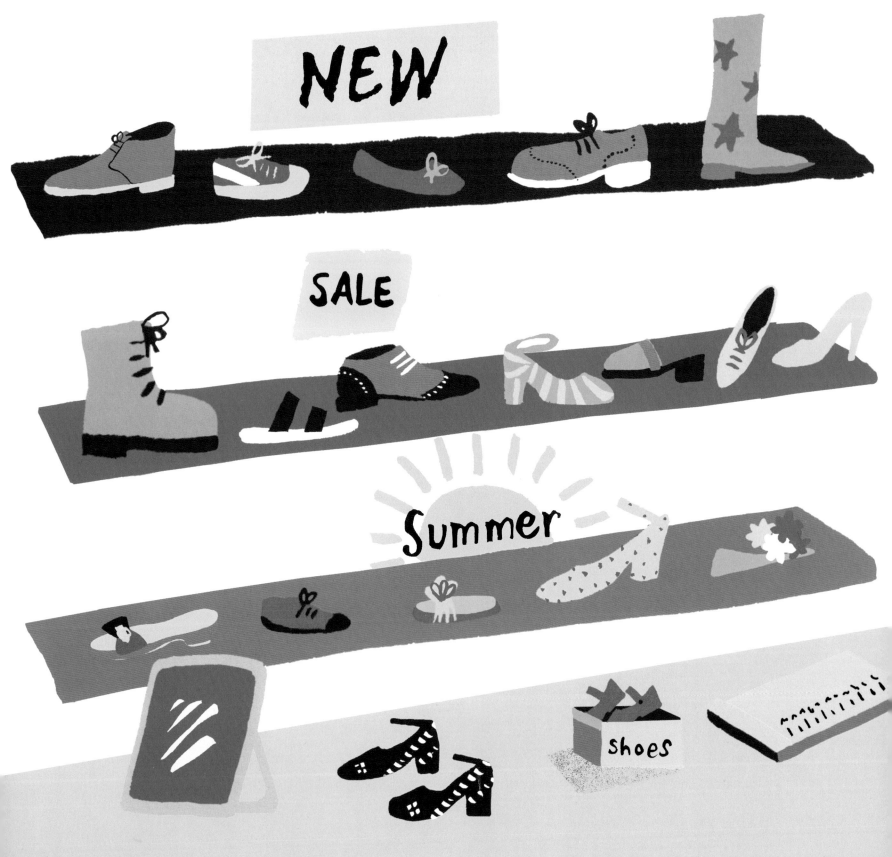

New shoes, shiny shoes,

Children's Shoes

rows and rows of different shoes.

Running shoes, sports shoes,

trying hard to win shoes.

Tap shoes, ballet shoes,

learning how to dance shoes.

Big shoes,

twinkly shoes,

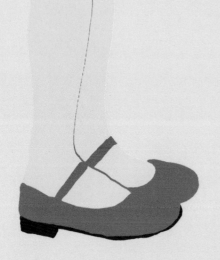

Mary Jane and boating shoes.

Tiny shoes,

lace-up shoes,

peekaboo and fluffy shoes.

Green shoes, purple shoes,

red, blue or yellow shoes!

New shoes, home shoes,

what to wear with new shoes.

Shoes, shoes, party shoes!

But best of all – OUR shoes!